This igloo book belongs to:

....

igloobooks

Published in 2020
First published in the UK by Igloo Books Ltd
An imprint of Igloo Books Ltd
Cottage Farm, NN6 0BJ, UK
Owned by Bonnier Books
Sveavägen 56, Stockholm, Sweden
www.igloobooks.com

1020 003
2 4 6 8 10 9 7 5 3
ISBN 978-1-83903-290-5

Written by Stephanie Moss
Illustrated by Junissa Bianda

Designed by Bethany Dowling
Edited by Caroline Richards

Printed and manufactured in China

BEDTIME STORIES

igloobooks

Contents

Little Stars

Emily and Phoebe had been pretending
to be explorers all afternoon.

SUPER
explorers

EXPLORER VEHICLE

SECRE
BOX

They were having so much fun in
their brand-new tent, they didn't notice
when the sun went down.

6

Suddenly, they heard a noise...

HOOT HOOT!

What's that?

asked Phoebe.
Then, there was a...

GRUMBLE RUMBLE!

I want to go inside!

But when they peered out of their tent, it was already dark.

7

Next, they heard a...

CRUNCH CRUNCH!

It got closer and closer until they heard a voice.

There's nothing to be scared of. Lots of things wake up at night.

EXPLORERS ONLY!

It was Phoebe's mummy, carrying a tray of treats!

Phoebe and Emily looked
outside and saw the owl
that had been hooting.

They even saw mice **creeping**
quietly in the grass and bats
swooping through the air.

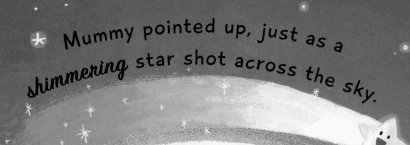

Mummy pointed up, just as a shimmering star shot across the sky.

Look, the Moon has woken up.

So have the stars.

Wow, it's magic!

10

Where's Teddy?

It was bedtime at Jake's house. He'd already had his bath, his warm milk from his sippy cup and even his favourite bedtime story. But he wouldn't go to sleep.

Someone very important was missing.

I'm not going to sleep. Not without Teddy.

Daddy tried bringing him Hippo, Tiger and Robot from the playroom instead, but Jake shook his head.

So Daddy and Jake searched the whole house. They looked
high and low, from here to there, but Teddy wasn't anywhere!

14

He wasn't in the washing basket and he wasn't in the wardrobe. He hadn't fallen under the table and Jake hadn't dropped him in the garden. Before long, Jake began to yawn.

So Daddy pulled back the covers and Jake climbed into bed.
There, already snuggled up in bed, was Teddy.

Jake **squealed** and gave him a great big cuddle.

See! Teddy was just ready for bed before you. Goodnight, Teddy. Goodnight, Jake,

whispered Daddy.

But Jake was already fast asleep.

The Mystery Monster

One night, when George was snuggled up fast asleep in his bed, he suddenly woke up.

I had a bad dream!

he cried out, but Mummy and Daddy didn't hear him.

So George got out of bed,
tiptoed across the carpet
and crept along the landing
to their bedroom.

Then George stopped
and looked behind him.

Something was
following him!

It was **big** and **dark**, with two arms and legs,
and when George moved, it moved, too!

George felt really scared and he stood very still...
then the something did as well.

Ahhh!
There's a monster following me!

shouted George, as loud as he could.

Just then, Mummy and Daddy came running out of their bedroom and gave George a big hug.

When George showed them the monster, Mummy smiled.

Don't worry, it's just your shadow. Look, there's mine!

They waved at their shadows on the wall.

George giggled as they waved back.

They had fun making shadow puppets on
the wall together until George started to feel
sleepy again. He yawned, and so did his shadow.

Goodnight, George.

Goodnight, Shadow!

The Magical Unicorn

Amy couldn't wait to stay over at Granny's house all on her own, but she was upset when she forgot to bring her favourite dolly.

What if I get scared?

Don't worry, I've got something very special for you.

On Amy's bed was a **super**-cuddly, **extra**-sparkly,
mega-rainbow unicorn! Secretly, Amy still missed her dolly,
but she kissed Granny and said goodnight.

Just then, something tickled Amy's nose. When she opened her eyes, the cuddly unicorn had come to life!

Before she knew it, they were flying through the air.

When they landed, Amy and the unicorn
were in a magical fairground!

She waved to the fairies as she watched them
ride the fairy coaster, and she **whooped** as she
swung on a swinging pirate ship!

27

Amy giggled all the way down the slippery rainbow slide...

... and she **whooshed** down a log flume that splashed into a mermaid lagoon.

It was so much fun, but she soon felt sleepy.

She yawned and, in a **flash**, she was back in bed.

I must tell Granny about the unicorn's magic.

Then, Granny looked around the door and whispered,

I already know. Goodnight, Amy.

29

Our Favourite Things

We have so much fun! Do you know what I like doing best?

asked Harry, as his dad tucked him into bed.

Dad chuckled. He could hardly choose just one thing!

Dad thought hard.
Harry always loved
playing at the park
and **whizzing**
through the air
on the swings.

Harry also loved it when Dad lifted
him up to ride on his shoulders.

Harry shook his head.

Is it helping me with my jobs?

Harry always joined in with baking a cake or cleaning the car, even if he did spray soapy water everywhere!

But Harry still said no.

Then it must be when we play noisy outdoor games!

Their favourite was football, and whenever Harry shouted,

GOAL!

... Dad laughed and covered his ears.

33

On rainy days Harry and Dad liked to play games.
Sometimes they did jigsaw puzzles together.

Harry and Dad even built big towers out
of bricks and **knocked** them down again.
Perhaps that's what Harry liked best?

Party Pyjamas

Holly had been invited to her first ever pyjama party, so she needed her best pyjamas. When she finally found them, there was a huge hole in them.

36

Holly was worried she wouldn't be able to go to the party at all.

Let's go shopping for some new ones,

said Mummy.

So they set off before the party started.

There were all kinds of different pyjamas.

Big ones and **small** ones, Spotty ones and stripy ones!

Mummy even found monster pyjamas
and rocket pyjamas...

... but Holly didn't like any of them.

Each time, she looked at her reflection in
the mirror and pulled a face.

I look silly.

Now Holly was sure she wouldn't
be able to go to the party!

Just then, the sales assistant came over, holding the *cutest* onesie Holly had ever seen. When Holly tried it on, it was like it was made for her.

SALE
20% OFF!

It's perfect!

When Holly arrived at the party,
her friends all gathered around.

Wow!

I love your onesie!

So cute!

It looks great!

Holly had such a good time, and she
couldn't wait for her next pyjama party.

Bedtime Tricks

When Anna, a new babysitter, came to look after Kitty and Kevin, they didn't feel like going to bed. So they changed the time on all the clocks to be one hour slow!

Kitty and Kevin ran off to play,
but a few minutes later, Anna called,

Bedtime!

Kitty checked the time, and all the clocks were right again.
Why hadn't their clever trick worked?

Let's try this instead,

said Kevin.

He pulled a **big**, hairy
toy spider out of their trick box!

They placed it carefully at the top of the stairs,
trying not to giggle.

They hid in the bathroom and waited for Anna's scream.
Instead, she walked in and asked,

Have you brushed
your teeth, yet?

Kitty and Kevin couldn't believe it.
Maybe Anna wasn't scared of spiders?

45

Kitty and Kevin felt disappointed, but they had run out of ideas. Kitty pulled back the covers and was about to get into bed, when she cried,

Ahhhhhhhh!

It was their trick spider!

At the same time, Kevin pulled back his own duvet and...

BOING!

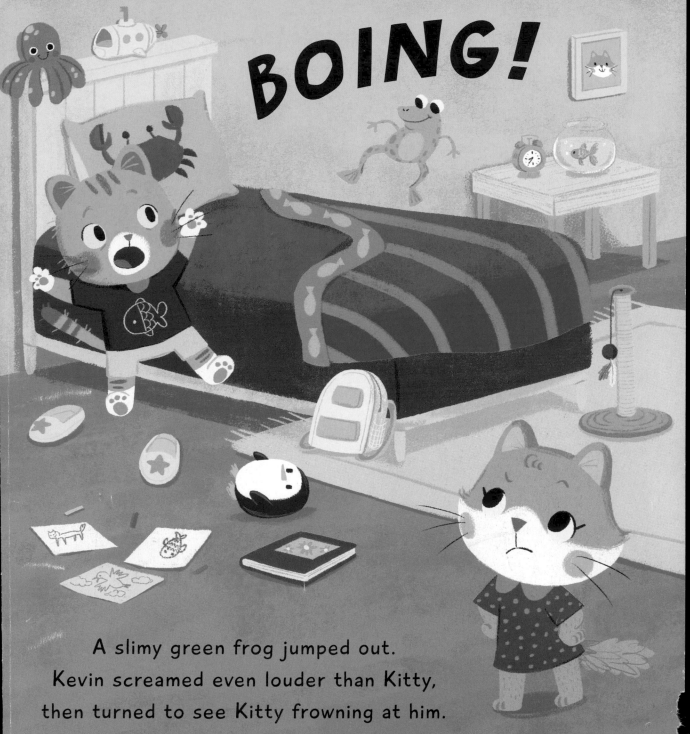

A slimy green frog jumped out.
Kevin screamed even louder than Kitty,
then turned to see Kitty frowning at him.

You tricked me!

they both shouted.

Just then, they heard
Anna, giggling.

No, I did. I loved
playing tricks when I
was your age. Especially
on my babysitters!